Flik to the Rescue

Adapted by Jane B. Mason

Disney PRESS

New York

Disney · PIXAR

a bug's life

Flik to the Rescue

Chapter 1

It was a busy day on Ant Island. Worker ants were busily harvesting grains of wheat to hand over when the grasshoppers arrived.

Each worker ant climbed up a stalk of wheat, plucked out a single grain, and carried it down to a large stone table near the anthill. The process went slowly. It took a l-o-n-g time. But the colony had been harvesting grain this way for as long as anyone could remember. So each ant climbed up and down, up and down.

Except for me, that is. My name is Flik.

1

You might say I'm an inventor. I'd just invented a contraption called a harvester. It harvested whole stalks of wheat at once! It could cut down the stalks, drop the wheat kernels in a basket, and toss the empty stalks out of the way.

I was moving through the wheat stalks with record speed. It was great! Stalks were falling down right and left around me. Then, all of a sudden, I heard an ant scream at me. Actually, it was a lot of ants.

"Hey!" the first one yelled.

"Look out!" called another.

"What do you think you're doing!" demanded a third.

Suddenly I realized that our queen and her whole council of advisers were shouting at me.

Uh-oh. I was in trouble again. I climbed down the grain stalk as fast as I could.

"I'm so sorry," I gasped as I hurried over to the Council. They were all standing around a fallen grain stalk, which had knocked over an unsuspecting ant. I tried to lift up the stalk. "Please forgive me. I, uh—"

That's when I noticed that it wasn't just any ant buried under the stalk. It was Princess Atta—the Queen's daughter!

"Flik, what are you doing?" Princess Atta demanded as her head popped out from under the stalk. Princess Atta is one of the prettiest ants in the colony. And one of the smartest. She was going to be queen one day.

I started to show her my harvester. But the rest of the Council was too busy worrying about the offering to listen. They kept mumbling about "no time" and "more important matters."

I couldn't blame them. The offering was scary because Hopper the leader of the grasshoppers was coming. Every year, he forced us to give him a huge offering of grain, and had promised to destroy our ant colony if we didn't please him. But even though my harvester could save so much time, they didn't listen to a word I said. They just sent me back to work!

How could I ever make a difference if nobody believed in me?

I didn't have much time to feel bad, though. A minute later the alarm bell sounded.

They were here!

Everyone panicked. Mobs of ants rushed toward the anthill.

As I hurried by the offering stone, I took off my harvester . . .

And it knocked into one of the legs on the altar.

The entire offering tumbled over the edge of the altar—and into the cracked riverbed surrounding Ant Island!

Chapter 2

I hurried into the anthill bunker.
Inside, ants huddled together,
trembling with fear. I rushed up
to Princess Atta. I had to tell her
what had happened!

"Princess Atta," I began. But
before I could say another
word, the chamber echoed
with a muffled buzzing sound. Footsteps
thundered above our heads.

"Hey, where's the food?" a nasty voice
shouted.

Everyone around me gasped in fear.

Atta's eyes went wide. "What did you do?" she asked me.

Just then giant feet shot through the ceiling and a gang of grasshoppers dropped through.

"So where is it?" Hopper asked. Hopper was a real bully. On top of that, he was mad. He had a scar on his face where he had been attacked by a bird. "WHERE'S MY FOOD!"

Atta went pale.

I felt terrible. Atta was training to take over for the Queen, and I was messing everything up for her. So when Hopper started picking on Atta's little sister, Princess Dot, I had to say something.

"Leave her alone!" I shouted. That was a big mistake.

"You ants seem to be forgetting your place," Hopper

growled. "I want double the order of food—before the last leaf falls!"

With a whoop, the grasshoppers buzzed away.

Everyone gasped. If we gave away more food, we'd starve!

Chapter 3

Luckily, I came up with a great idea. What the colony needed was some help— some warrior bugs to fight off the grasshopper bullies.

Of course, to find warriors one of us would have to leave Ant Island. Since it was my idea, I volunteered.

I didn't think they'd let me go. Nobody *ever* leaves Ant Island. But they agreed. Actually, it was Atta who agreed. Like I said, she's one smart ant.

It was a long journey, but I finally arrived. The city! It was even more exciting than I'd dreamed. There were bugs everywhere— bugs I'd never even heard of before. It was amazing!

I made my way to a rough-looking bar. It wasn't the kind of place I'd usually hang out in, but I was looking for some tough bugs. And let me tell you, I found 'em.

Right in the middle of the bar were the fiercest bugs I'd ever seen. A ladybug and a caterpillar were in a heated sword fight against some flies.

"You have robbed from the poor for too long!" the ladybug declared.

Before I knew it, the whole bar tipped over and rolled down the street. These were serious warrior bugs!

I didn't waste any time. I walked right up

to those bugs and spoke my mind. "You guys were 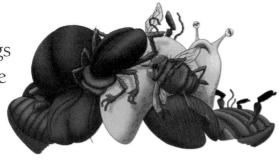 GREAT!" I told them. "I've been scouting all over for bugs with your kind of talent!" Then I made my offer.

"I'm from an ant colony just east of here, and some grasshoppers are coming at the end of the season. We're really low on food and we don't know what to do. Would you guys be willing to come and help us—"

I didn't even have to finish explaining our situation. The warriors ushered me out of the bar. The next thing I knew, we were flying back to Ant Island.

I rode on the back of the big beetle called Dim. The two pill bugs, Tuck and Roll, rode with me. Before long we were back at Ant Island.

We arrived just in time. The ants at the colony were exhausted from all the harvesting work.

Dot saw me first. She waved excitedly. But as we landed, the rest of the ants screamed and ran. I guess we looked pretty scary.

"Tah-dah!" The warrior bugs struck a fancy warrior pose.

"Hey, everybody!" I called as I slid off Dim's back. "I'm back! Look who's here with me!" The timid ant colony gathered around.

Dot believed me. But the rest of the ants looked surprised. They were excited, though, when the warriors showed their stuff. The ant children admired Dim, who looked like a tank. His trainer, Rosie the spider, shooed them away when they tickled him. Francis, a ladybug, grabbed the walking stick Slim and whacked Heimlich the caterpillar over the head while the acrobats Tuck and Roll executed a quick flip. Then, as Manny the mantis magician waved his hands, Gypsy flashed the scary "eyes" on her moth wings. The ant crowd gave a long, drawn-out "Ooooh!"

"They're our ticket out of this mess," one of the Council members said.

"They came just in time!" another added.

"That's right!" chimed in a third.

Finally, I'd done something right!

Chapter 4

 That afternoon we held a giant banquet to welcome the warriors. It was amazing!

A group of kids from the ant colony elementary school put on a play for our heroes.

"I tell you a tale of heroes so bold, who vanquished our grasshopper enemies of old," a Council member narrated.

Little ants dressed up as grasshoppers battled little ants dressed up as warrior bugs.

". . . I die! Die! Die!" one of the ant children dressed up as a warrior exclaimed. He fell to the ground with a *thud.*

What a play! The warriors were so entertained, they almost fainted.

When it was over, Princess Atta got up to make a speech. She was so nervous, no one could hear her, so I made her a megaphone out of a leaf.

Atta thanked the warrior bugs for coming to help us. And then she thanked me! I was so excited I jumped right onstage. I had to thank *her.* I mean, she was the one who agreed to let me go on my quest. Without Princess Atta, none of this would have happened!

I was in the middle of my speech when Rosie the black widow spider whispered something in my ear. She said: "Flik, we're *circus* bugs."

It took a minute for her words to sink in. I gulped. Then I took the megaphone and spoke to the Princess.

"The warriors have called a secret meeting so they can trapeze—ah, trap the grasshoppers with ease!" I lied. Then I ushered the circus bugs out of there as fast as I could.

Once we were hidden, I lost my temper. "Circus bugs? I thought you were warriors! You said you were gonna break legs! You were gonna knock grasshoppers dead! This, my friends, is false advertising!"

I guess that made the bugs pretty mad, because they turned on their multiple legs and walked away.

I had to convince them to stay. If I didn't, the ant colony would find out the truth. I'd be branded a loser forever!

I chased after the circus bugs. I begged. I pleaded. As they flew off the island, I grabbed Slim's legs.

We all landed across the riverbed from Ant Island. "Let go!" Slim exclaimed. I felt bad for hurting him. But I was desperate.

"No!" I shouted. Then I saw something that made me change my mind. Something terrifying.

A bird!

Chapter 5

I let go of Slim in a hurry and ran for my life.

"Run!" I shouted to circus bugs.

The bird let out a loud screech. It chased after the bugs. They leaped off the island into the riverbed.

I heard someone call my name. "Flik!" Overhead, little Dot was floating through the sky riding a dandelion puff. She must have followed us.

SCREEEEECH! The bird dived right toward her.

Dot let go of the puff just in time. But now she was tumbling toward the ground—fast!

"I gotcha!" Francis caught Dot at the last second. But then the two of them fell into a deep crack in the ground. And the bird was still after them!

I was hiding behind a giant rock with the circus bugs.

"Oh, no!" one of them said.

"We've got to do something!" added another.

I had to think fast. "Oh!" I suddenly said. "I've got an idea!"

My plan was risky, but we didn't have a choice. While Slim the walking stick and Heimlich the caterpillar used themselves as bait, the rest of us rescued Dot and Francis.

Everything went fine . . . until it was time for Heimlich to escape into a crack in the riverbed. He was too fat to fit!

"Help!" he shouted. "I'm stuck!"

The bird let out another screech and soared toward the caterpillar. Just as it was about to eat Heimlich alive, Gypsy the moth

distracted the bird with the scary face on her wings. The caterpillar sucked in his belly and disappeared into the crack.

We were carrying Dot to safety when the bird spotted us. We were right next to a cliff! We flew into a thorn bush just in time.

As we all sighed in relief, we heard a strange sound.

The colony was clapping and cheering! The ants had seen the whole thing. We were heroes!

Chapter 6

Francis had
broken his
leg in the
gorge, so
we took him to the infirmary. It wasn't long
before the Blueberries showed up. The
Blueberries is a club for little girls, and Dot is
their youngest member.

I was still trying to think of a way to get
the circus bugs to stay. Even though they
weren't really warriors, I had a feeling they
could help us. Especially when Atta

reminded me that Hopper was afraid of birds.

"This is perfect!" I told the bugs. "We can get rid of Hopper, and no one has to know that I screwed up. You'll even be gone  before the grasshoppers arrive!"

I started to tell them the actual plan, but Manny the praying mantis cut me off.

"We'll have no part of it!" he declared.

That's when a couple of ant boys came into the infirmary. They wanted the bugs' autographs!

Manny was so flattered he forgot all about having no part of my great plan.

The circus bugs were going to help after all!

Later that afternoon, the colony gathered in the anthill courtroom. Manny stood in the

center, explaining THE GREAT PLAN. It was my plan, of course. But if we told the colony that, they'd never agree. They would never trust me to have an idea as important as this.

"We're going to build a bird that we can operate from the inside," Manny explained. "It will be hoisted above the anthill and hidden high in the tree."

While Manny talked, I looked around at my fellow ants. My plan was very unusual. It wasn't the kind of thing our colony did. It was even dangerous.

I was worried that the Council wouldn't go for it. But Princess Atta came through for me.

"It's going to take everyone's involvement to make this plan a reality," she told the colony. "I know it's not our tradition to do things differently. But if our ancestors were able to build this anthill, we can certainly rally together to build this bird."

Everyone cheered for the second time that day. Maybe, finally, we could get rid of the grasshoppers for good!

Chapter 7

First we cut out the shape of the bird from a big leaf. Then we positioned it between the sun and the ground so it made a giant shadow.

"Okay!" Princess Atta shouted through her megaphone. "Hit your marks!"

Groups of ants rushed forward, carrying sticks. Using the shadow as a guide, they shaped the outline of the bird. Then came the backbone, the wings, and the tail. Rosie

used her spider-
webbing to
tie every-
thing togeth-
er. We cov-
ered the whole
thing with leaves. They looked just like
feathers.

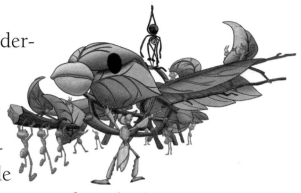

When the bird was complete, a troop of
ants climbed inside to test the wings.

"That's the way. Put your backs into it!"
Manny called out. "Up . . . down . . . up . . .
down . . . "

It worked!

It took a l-o-n-g rope and a lot of team-
work to get the bird into the hollow. But with
all of us pulling together, we managed to do
it. We set the bird on a launching rack.

Our bird was ready for takeoff! To celebrate,
we threw a party. There was a giant conga line
and lots of food. Everyone had a good time.

I stepped up to the circus bugs. "When the

party quiets down, I'll sneak you out the back way—and you're outta here forever." I would be sad to see the bugs go, but a deal was a deal.

Dim spoke first. "Dim don't want to go," he said.

"Well, if Dim stays . . . " Rosie began.

"I promised the Blueberries I'd teach them canasta," added Francis.

Gypsy beamed. "It seems we've been booked for an extended engagement!"

I didn't know what to say. Our circus bugs wanted to stay!

Just then the alarm siren sounded. The grasshoppers were coming!

"Battle stations, everyone!" Atta instructed. "This is not a drill!"

Each ant knew exactly what to do. But instead of a gang of grasshoppers, a circus train arrived.

"I am the great P. T. Flea!" the driver called out. "I'm the boss of this outfit, and I'm looking for some of my circus performers."

A couple of fireflies unrolled posters. They showed pictures of our warrior bugs!

I stepped forward in a hurry. I couldn't let the ants find out the truth!

"No, no, no," I declared. "Sorry, but I've never seen anyone like that around here."

But one of the Council members was right behind me—and he recognized Slim! A second later P. T. spotted his troupe. They were sneaking away under a leaf.

Atta stepped up to the bugs. "You mean you're not warriors?" she asked.

"Are you kiddin'?" P. T. replied. "These guys are the lousiest circus bugs you've ever seen."

The Council was horrified. "You mean our

entire defensive strategy was concocted by clowns?!!"

"Hey!" Francis shouted in defense. "We really thought Flik's idea was going to work!"

Things really went downhill from there. Everyone was furious with me. I tried to convince them that the bird could still work. It could save us—even if it was another one of my nutty ideas.

Nobody believed me, though. Not even Princess Atta.

"You lied to me," she said. "And like an idiot I believed you." Atta's beautiful eyes were full of tears. "I want you to leave, Flik," she told me. "And this time, don't come back."

Chapter 8

I wanted to argue, but
I knew it was no use.
The whole colony had
turned against me. So
I just climbed into
the circus cart with
the rest of the bugs.

As P. T. drove the cart through the dark-
ness, the bugs tried to cheer me up. But I felt
terrible. I wanted to crawl into a crack in the
circus cart and stay there forever.

All of a sudden, I heard someone call my
name. "Flik! Wait!"

A moment later Dot landed on the back of the cart. She looked exhausted. "You have to come back," she panted. "Hopper came back. His gang is eating everything! And when they're finished, Hopper's going to squish my mom!"

All the bugs were horrified.

"What should we do?"

"The bird!"

"Yes! Of course! The bird will work!"

I turned away. "Let's face it," I told them. "That bird is a guaranteed failure. Just like me."

I was feeling even worse than before. But the bugs wouldn't give up. They reminded me that I wasn't a failure. I had succeeded in bringing out the best in them.

Soon I realized something. Dot really *did* believe in me. And so did the bugs.

I got to my feet. "Let's do it!"

Chapter 9

As soon as we got back to the anthill, we put our plan into action.

A bright light pierced the night, right in front of Hopper. The bugs put on a circus performance to distract the grasshoppers.

Meanwhile, I climbed up to the bird with a group of Blueberries. Then we waited for Gypsy the moth to give the signal.

"This is it, girls!" I told the Blueberries. "Get ready to roll!"

At the right moment, the bird zoomed out of the tree. *SCREEECH!*

Hopper looked up. "Ahhh! A bird!"

The grasshoppers screamed and ran.

Our plan was working!

Then, all of a sudden, there was smoke inside the bird! Someone must have set it on fire!

I cut the emergency cord, and the bird crashed to the ground. Luckily, everyone was safe. But when Dot climbed out of the bird, Hopper swooped in and grabbed her.

"Put her down, Hopper!" I shouted. "I'm the one you want."

Hopper dropped Dot, but he unleashed a vicious grasshopper on me!

"Let this be a lesson to all you ants," Hopper told everyone. "You are losers, put on this earth to serve us!"

I was in agony, but Hopper was really

making me mad. I had to prove that he was wrong! I got to my feet. "These ants somehow manage to pick food for themselves AND you," I said. "We're a lot stronger than you say we are!"

Hopper knew I was right, and that made him *really* mad. He knocked me down. But as I landed with a *thud*, something amazing happened. All the ants banded together and stood up to the grasshoppers. And Hopper was afraid!

"Get back!" he shouted.

Atta knew just what to do.

Charge!

Chapter 10

The ants and the circus bugs charged the grasshoppers like you wouldn't believe.

"Yaaaahh!"

"Take that!"

"Tickle them, girls!" Francis called to the Blueberries.

It was a great battle. The grasshopper gang knew when they were beaten. They began to flee, leaving Hopper alone to face us. Together we grabbed Hopper and loaded him into a cannon. We were about to send him on his way when it started to rain.

The drops exploded on the ground like giant meteors. Atta and I were still reeling from the raindrops when Hopper grabbed me and flew up into the branches of the tree.

The circus bugs tried to follow us, but the rain hampered them.

Then my heroine came through. Atta flew up, grabbed me away from Hopper, and carried me to the riverbank.

That's when I got my idea. Lure Hopper to the bird's nest!

Atta and I moved as quickly as we could. Rain pounded down on us, and Hopper was hot on our trail. But we kept going.

When we got to the right place, I hid Atta behind a leaf. "No matter what happens, stay here!" I told her.

I backed closer and closer to the nest, luring Hopper toward it. "H-Hopper! I didn't mean it! Please, don't!" I shouted as loud as I could. I had to wake up the bird!

Hopper was getting closer and closer. In another second he'd have me!

SKREEEE! The bird let out a shriek.

Hopper looked up and smiled. "Another one of your little bird tricks?" he jeered.

"No. It's real," I told him. And then I ran back to Atta.

The bird swooped down. It grasped Hopper in its beak.

A moment later, the bird babies had a very yummy meal.

Chapter 11

With the grasshoppers
gone for good, the ant
colony was a happy
place. The ants and cir-
cus bugs worked togeth-
er and played together.

Before long, all the worker ants were outfitted
with my harvesters!

But soon it was time to say good-bye to
our circus friends. P. T. Flea had given them
a fair circus contract. Performances would be
starting up soon.

We were sad to see them go, but they promised they'd all be back to visit.

"All right, everybody!" P. T. shouted anxiously. "We're outta here!"

As the circus wagon pulled away, we all waved.

The bugs waved back excitedly. "Farewell, Flik! 'Bye, Flik! Byesky, Fleek! Auf Wiedersehen, Flik!" Heimlich the plump caterpillar had turned into a plump butterfly. He got off the ground—barely.

I was thinking how silly they looked when Atta leaned in close to my ear.

"Uh, Flik, honey?" she asked sweetly.

I blushed. Did I mention that Princess Atta is the prettiest ant in the colony?

"Yes?" I answered.

"How on earth did you *ever* think they were warriors?"

The circus cart disappeared from sight. I smiled. It was the best mistake I'd ever made.

CATCH THE BUZZ!

Look for more *A Bug's Life* books in stores now

A Bug's Life Classic Storybook
(also available in Spanish)

A Bug's Life:
Can You Find the Difference?

A Bug's Life:
Special Collector's Edi

The Quest for the
One Big Thing

A Bug's Life
Flip Book

A Bug's Life
Junior Nov